I0630677

Edition BAES

www.edition-baes.com

Deutsche Fassung erschienen bei skarabäus, Innsbruck 2007

Übersetzung: Isabelle Esser
Cover: Peter Feller
Layout: Alexander Augustin · buechermacher.at

Herstellung: Books on Demand GmbH, Norderstedt

ISBN 978-3-9503811-8-4

Elias Schneitter

Moments of a biography in which
Giorgio Voghera
puts in several appearances.

*Set in Trieste, Rome, Vienna, Zirl
and Lowell Massachusetts – a promenade
through the world of a literature
whose aim is not the story
but the narrative.*

Edition BAES

phoneme calling grapheme
could be a brief yet misguided start,
even though the image isn't that bad
but where did i pick up this odd couple,
in trieste, in rome, vienna, lowell massachusetts,
or did they drift into my mind
at home in bed
one sleepless night?
it doesn't really matter
anyway.
i don't know.
phoneme and grapheme,
this mysteriously obscure couple,
i naïvely wonder whether
they found each other
like two young lovers:
phoneme and grapheme,
now an old familiar couple,
that turned my head so completely
that i often don't know what to do
as oskar pastior once said
after a lecture.

many thanks for your order,
i read in an email on my computer
from a German antiquarian,

unfortunately yesterday,
we sold our only copy of *the secret*
by the anonimo triestino.
so disappointed by this news,
i order a pile of poetry books,
some with inscriptions,
which don't usually impress me,
by the old beatnik warhorses:
huncke, bremser, corso, ginsberg, sanders,
wieners, plymell, vega,
many of them from the cherry valley near new york.
relieved, I go into town,
past bozner platz and i order in my "mind"
a mineral water, and only then does it dawn on me
how much these books will cost me.
a few days pass
before I try again,
trawling the net
for the book by the anonimo triestino.

at home in our village they sit in a dark café:
victor, roman, and a third,
they're poring over sentence structures.
roman clears his throat,
staring into the screen of a laptop,
pensive:
chomsky and generative grammar,
says victor, 64 sentence structures to work with

and completely arbitrary,
the random generator
this computerized writer.
they're filling the word pots:
names, places,
localities,
people from the past,
the present, and it wouldn't be so bad,
they say, if it wasn't for those *verbs,*
the agreement with the objects,
the adverbs,
making sure the computerized writer
comes up with some hits,
with complete comprehensible sentences.
they gaze at the laptop
fascinated,
sentence after sentence pouring out,
the writing program they developed
writes and composes
in this dark, dark bar,
that isn't really made for poetry,
but more for hardened drinkers.

filled pots of words
programmed syntactic structures
generated with random

slowly this product is turning into something,
i tell my dear old friend,
the poet of the café central, who is a little under the
weather
and asks: but what's it for?
for developing a computer that writes its own poetry,
is the answer,
and to mark the twelve hundredth anniversary of
the local village,
someone reads from the digital local history book.

a poetry computer
a mechanical writer
on endless paper

we are not of this world we once read
in a old script,
with the following side notes
added by hand:
all just borrowed
all just placed at our disposal
not made by our hand.
but
always these sentences,
always these scraps,
always these combinations
always this confusion
always rome, always vienna, always trieste,

always lowell massachusetts,
or just at home,
always at home, confined within our own four walls,
or even in the beloved golden light
of san francisco,
that we know only from hearsay,
as the computer program confirms.

all that men want is to spread
their seed around,
i hear a woman saying on the table next to me,
women only want security
and they even want the copyright
on men's semen.
it's saturday morning,
i'm reading the weekend edition
in the café tyrolis
and i can't help but hear,
i don't look up,
and i'm not particularly interested,
but somehow it drifts across to me,
because somehow it always drifts over,
i don't know why.
perhaps because of the copyright,
which has been nagging me
for years.

book in hand and all alone
i walked one night
the long way from the bowery
into 454 w. 20th st,
to linger in front of this silent house for a while,
opposite the red brick church,
before walking back,
past the corner of 7th avenue,
on to penn station and into my hotel,
where i fell into bed, exhausted and happy.

a sentence in a book
who does it belong to?
the author?
the reader?
the publisher?
the shelf it's standing on?
or the paper it's printed on?
what do you think?
what about ownership,
and copyright?

or:
are sentences the same as
cabbages in a vegetable patch,
that can be attributed mostly to the gardener?
or do they belong to the person,
whose pot they're cooking in?

is this something you ever think about?
does it even interest you?

god is never on the side of the perpetrator,
but always of the victim,
my friend, the buddhist, said
after we had spent all night
whiling away the hours
in various bars in the railroad viaduct.
could god be seen as a perpetrator,
we asked ourselves as the night progressed,
could all this shit actually be *his* fault,
we say, talking over our early morning drink.
of course, we also knew:
the later the evening, the more beautiful the guests.
that's the truth.
so we went to the witch's kitchen, where they say:
admission costs three hooks to the jaw and a knife
in the back.
you can get cheap hot dogs with potato salad
there
and when you leave,
and get home
your wife knows,
exactly where you've been
because you stink of fries and rancid oil,
but at least you don't have a knife in your back,
which I guess is progress.

in the same way that you haven't had a wife for
some time now,
times change,
because everything's going to be alright,
as the lord our father keeps telling us.

since my separation
i've been chasing something
or running away from it.
this entry sticks in his head
for quite some time, for he
doesn't know which way to turn,
wandering from one bar in trieste
to the next,
only to end up in the san marco.
he takes a seat across from where
giorgio voghera always sits,
and where by coincidence one of his sisters
is immersed in quiet conversation with claudio
magris.
he can't understand a single word,
and that feels good,
not only because he's had too much to drink.

phoneme and grapheme.
do sentences have a gender,
breasts or an ass?
are syntactic structures genetic occurrences,

can sentences cancel each other out
or should they just be swallowed?
it is clear that when a sentence fossilizes,
its job is done.
it returns home.
as long as it still lives in us,
it is not dead.
dead sentences are ash in our heads,
there is plenty of space in there for that.
a viennese german philologist uses these metaphors
in a celebratory address
about the baroque in austrian
literature after the second world war.

near rome in the park aviary
i seriously try
to put pen to paper for her
to write about
my childhood and the disease of my youth,
just as i'd promised this hopeless love
on the telephone.
but as i write
self-pity and the gravity of it all have me
firmly in their clutches,
so much so
that nothing worth reading
could possibly come out of my writing utensil.
perhaps i should get together with victor

and his computer after all,
i'm left with this thought in the park aviary,
where the screeching birds in the wind
sound like rusty bicycle chains.

where can you travel when you're single?
where can you go on your own?
where can you stay all alone?
where can you go to kill time?
in truth, you never travel alone,
there's always some alter ego tagging along,
searching for excuses as you make
your travel plans.
at least the child-ego
and the parent-ego are always with you.
in fact, a whole busload of egos,
a multiple ego trip,
never budging from the group,
the brochure pokes fun at
the travelers,
who don't even notice,
because they're so fixated on the price.
hopefully the strain of traveling
won't be too much for any of the egos,
is the thought,
as the organism
stands at a blue metallic bar,
the mind wandering to far-off cities.

it's late, the town is empty.
heading for home,
thinking it would be nice
to have someone waiting there,
someone to lean on,
without having to talk,
because when we reach a certain age
we can't expect too much,
which is why night-time TV keeps us company
as we drift off to sleep.

i'm not quite ready yet,
standing in the plaza
outside the internal revenue building
where at this time of day
the world is still all right
i greet other night owls,
who I've known for a very long time.
we smile at each other knowingly,
there's no need to speak,
a nod says it all.

always these money worries,
always out of cash,
always short,
always in overdraught,
always never free from it all,

always never solvent:
it's such a shame,
such a shame,
laments a poet
after his trip to rome
one day in café katzung.

changing the topic:
what about the chosen narrative:
rising above things.
the plot: pure invention.
the characters: very complex, not always authentic.
the subject matter, the motifs, the locations of the plot,
all finely woven, well thought-through,
not a letter too much,
not a sentence too few,
no chapter wasted.
in a nutshell: enchanting
all in all.
though perhaps rising a little too much above everything.
otherwise a work
not to be sneezed at.
i understand only too well,
that women find me impossible to live with,
after all, i find it
impossible to live with myself.
in the same way that i

don't trust a single soul,
not since i realized,
i can't trust myself.
i learned that from my grandfather.
just a quick question though in between:
what does christmas mean to you
and doesn't every day mark the advent of a new year?

phoneme calling grapheme
we really don't want to know
what will become of them.
but damn the syntax,
the grammar,
the spelling,
and those stupid phrases about
composing
beautiful sentences
and having a polished style,
scipio slataper said for posterity.
i much prefer the kind of writing
that's all over the place,
because writing, said scipio, must be
a barbaric act,
how else can it come from a torn and broken soul.
soon after he himself went off to war,
and a bullet
extinguished his light.

i'm firmly planted with both feet next to my life,
says my friend hubert by the village square,
as he slips off his shoes
and stands next to them.

we find ourselves in some sleazy joint.
as he gets up to go,
one of the patrons says:
i'm leaving you and all your misery behind me.

oh god: why can't i
live this love,
worship this woman,
taste her skin,
kiss her mouth,
feel her body,
look at her through dreamy eyes,
go dancing with her,
stroll through the city hand in hand,
know she's lying next to me at night,
booms a slightly ageing gentleman
from the stage of the local theater;
choosing to miss
the second half,
the spectator leaves the theater quite deflated.
five years have passed since they broke up,
he remembers,
before descending into the subway

and traveling to the roma termini,
taking the commuter train
into the suburbs,
where he treats himself to a portion of spaghetti limone,
the words still lingering in his memory,
giving him hope again.
and now for the retrospection
from the roman days:
at the age of nine, a child was admitted
for surgery to the university clinic
to correct a squint.
an author starts
jotting down the text with a pencil
in a large notebook.
colorful fish had been painted
on the ceiling of the children's ward,
he continues,
and after the dressing
was removed from the child's eyes
three days later,
he saw each of the fish double.
the author pauses,
something inside him refuses
to write on about diplopia,
or double vision.
he puts the notebook to one side,
stands up,
goes into the kitchen,

his friend and his girlfriend
are cooking spaghetti.
how are you getting on with your piece?
the friend asks, offering him a glass of wine.
it wouldn't be so bad, replies the author,
but i'm having problems, getting my hand
to write it. there's a block inside me,
even though i only have to write it down.
i know how you feel, says the friend,
maybe it'll get easier
after a glass of wine
and some spaghetti limone.

by avoiding society,
you step outside society,
and standing outside society
is the essence of beat, says jack in the bowery
to his friend john clellon holmes,
who appears to take it
more seriously than kerouac,
after all, he's in the middle of the *go* manuscript,
which appears two years later
and amazes jack
and prompts him,
in a three-week sprint to the finish
in the confines of 454w. 20th st
to type his fourth version of *on the road*
onto a forty-meter long tele-typing roll,

all in one go,
sweating his way through a dozen t-shirts
and doped up with benzedrine
and coffee.

i just bought a notebook
and a fineliner, because you never know
which letters will be blown
your way during the day.
besides, i still write best
sober, out in the street,
in my head and without a pad,
these lines i write on a postcard
with my new black fineliner and i send them
to eduard-hanslick-gasse
in the 16th district of vienna.

at any rate: the linear storyline is
as much an invention as the right angle.
in real life neither exists.
which is why both seem so false
and none of the greek temples have right angles,
i hear a voice piping up in the passenger seat,
on our way to trieste.
never trust an architect
who embraces right angles,
my father used to joke,
but he would know.

does life unravel like a story,
like a narrative,
or is it just a fiction of the desk,
the poet at the café central asks me.
why are you putting that question
to me of all people?
i retort,
ordering another small
beer and a chaser to follow,
because i don't want to go home
to my tv.
what's the view of the office worker?
my friend continues to probe.
when will this idiotic syntax,
this shit grammar finally end.
when can we finally just write and write,
without worrying about commas and punctuation
without the dogma of the sentence
that sits well,
polished on the grindstone of schoolbook grammar.
that's all that remains of the evening
with the poet at the café central.

when will
the yelling and bawling arrive on paper,
without the germanic shackles,
without the nooses,
without the orderly rows

all in tune, spouts a youthful poet
in the beer garden, beer mug in hand
in front of his colleagues,
who find his speech highly amusing,
and certainly don't take him seriously,
for all he has are a few photocopied poems
none of which have been published.
when will the *phoneme* finally find the *grapheme*,
beyond the desks,
shouts someone,
who's the spitting image of
peter vonstadel.
and while we're on the topic,
he continues wearily,
the old joyce who uttered obscurities
to his surroundings,
was the best joyce
there ever was,
even though it doesn't matter anymore,
because it was so long ago.

i'm thinking of my distant unknown heritage,
of my ancestors and their background,
this is typed with grim determination
into the computer
which constantly crashes
because too many programs are hampering work.
but they're all necessary,

because anything could happen
and you have to prepare
for all eventualities.
more than twelve hundred years ago,
the text continues,
this race
migrated from the coast of the Dutch mud flats
down into the mountains.
the reasons can be explained.

the potato or spud,
it was said in grandma's kitchen,
was *the blessing of the earth.*
the potato as the epitome of life:
full of expectation in the spring,
when the seed was planted in the soil –
full of melancholy in the autumn,
when the wonderfully sour fragrance
of the burned potato plants
lingered in the air
over the village
and the potatoes disappeared
into the cooling cellar rooms
and a sense of calm
descended upon the farmhouse.
grandma's strict gaze still
ubiquitous.
she, the guardian of the filled storage rooms.

with those bad eyes,
that double view of the world,
it was bound to go wrong in the end.
the years
as grandma's world was dissolving
and after the annual trips
to the united states,
to lowell, orlando, northport,
jacksonville florida,
that dark place,
san francisco, monterey, san pedro, salinas
and back up to northbeach,
it was all years ago
and the bitter memory
of the deaths that catch up with us:
jack micheline, kathy acker, jan kerouac,
ray bremser, richard brautigan, john wieners,
gregory corso, buk, philip whalen,
from one moment to the next
the clock just stopped ticking,
though time marched on.
and so the yearning for trieste
becomes more understandable,
not only because it's closer,
no, it's the sea,
the winds,
the bora from the lowlands
the scirocco blowing up from the sea

and the idiocy of the irredentists,
decades later
in a very different way:

just a word about art.
perhaps you could help.
my research program
raises questions:
who was the first to sign a work of art?
where did it happen?
was it the start of manic individualism?
could you do me a favor and
send appropriate suggestions in confidence
to the publisher?
all the best for your past
i wish you on new year's eve.
and we know from political circles
in china: indicate left and go right,
full stop

my writing must be more pleasing on the eye,
a voice nags me deep from within
echoing around my study,
relentless.
you must understand that letters
emerge from flesh and blood.
the question is:
how are they infused

with flesh and blood,
once they're on paper?
always be on your toes
always stay on the scent,
like urs mannhart in *luchs*.
filling letters with flesh and blood
is the author's responsibility,
or so christoph simon
tells me with an ironic smile.
sitting on the veranda in front of my house,
drinking cheap schnapps,
he throws a quick sketch in his notebook,
to avoid using letters.
christoph knows of my scientific efforts
in the realm of copyright,
so he avoids
writing anything down in my presence.
weeks later he sends me
a sheet of paper with a drawing,
which he calls *the portrait of the alphabet*.

on ponte rosso in trieste – where
for my own entertainment
i start searching for reasons – i suddenly
realize my hero is an irredentist for women,
rejected and exiled, although he himself
had always thought of fleeing,
like this city,

whose longing represented a redemption
that it never got to grips
with,
though it was to add to its uniqueness.
anyway while standing on ponte rosso
i come up with the following summary:
seeing double
like a drunkard,
my brain cannot
deliver identical images,
as the health report on tv
confirms,
but this information
is too much of a platitude,
to be pursued any further.

many years later, in late summer, i'm standing
in trieste in an antiquarian bookstore in the old jewish
quarter and i ask the sales assistant:
c'è il libro il *segreto* dell'anonimo triestino, per favore?
and the young sales assistant
looks at me astonished,
goes to a shelf, grabs the book
and just as i want to pay,
he stops me and says smiling
è l'ultimo ed è un regalo
per lei.

at times mozart's music can really
get on your nerves
making you appreciate schönberg,
says an old member of the vienna boys' choir
during a boozy evening of mulled wine
and chestnuts just north of merino.
great art, he continues,
always seeps through the cracks,
concludes his old school friend franz schuh,
whom he greatly admires.

but on ponte rosso it suddenly occurs to me,
after eating a pizza,
why i feel drawn to trieste,
pulled toward the old and new harbors,
and to muggia,
back to the sea.
it must have something to do with my ancestors,
who left the sea twelve hundred years ago,
only to end up in the mountains,
and whose longing pervades my organism.
otherwise the pull of the sea would not be so strong,
and so my thoughts wander
as i cross ponte rosso in trieste.

after twelve hundred years i still
can't get used to the mountains,
i tell a fortune teller in fassergassse in hall,

who doesn't know what to make of this information
gazing out of the window pensively for a very long
time,
across to the bettelwurf mountain.
to break the silence,
i tell a story
that starts like this:
i never really liked stories
such as these,
i say,
such as the one
about my uncle,
who kept a piton and a carabiner
in his room
showing them to all his visitors,
because they had once saved his life
when mountaineering on martin's rock face.
stories like these give me goose bumps,
i say.
if i could i would erase these tales
from my memory,
but that appears impossible,
if you know,
what i mean.

send *me* a postcard
when *you* are feeling down,
just to make me feel a little better.

because we know
what people are like,
without having to point
the finger.

for me trieste is a climatic compromise,
i tell veit heinichen in his vineyard
above the bay of grignano.
we drink plum schnapps,
his favorite tipple
in the schnapps department.
he's always working hard,
has little time to spare.
he originates from swabia
and knows nothing of pirates and seafarers
in his ancestry.
even so, he still lives in trieste.

by the way, one should add,
we are told
that novels can only be seen
as fossils from a bygone age.
no sooner has this quote been read,
to which veit heinichen incidentally laughed
out loud, than peter is
sitting at a small marble table saying:
i'm having unbearable withdrawal symptoms
from the chemo...

the waiter brings him a bottle of beer
and peter says in a meek voice:
as of now i'm no longer here,
or part of my body.
the doctors are extending its sell by date.

then a patron gets up,
in a hurry.
leaving his drink,
he goes out
into the square,
toward maria-theresien-straße
and suddenly a thought springs to mind,
that the i in a book

and the i in life
are two completely different things.
but to know that
you don't need
a literature degree.
grasping it, of course,
is different again.
how can a story continue?
or in other words:
how can a story begin?
do stories come down
from extraterrestrial transmitter stations,
operated by agents?

are letters
messages from distant galaxies?
is a pencil stroke on a sheet of paper
a message from unknown occupying forces?
or as my son klaus once asked,
cereal bar in hand
at the seiser alm,
while a busload of german tourists
marched loudly past:
dad, how does it work with all those letters in our
heads?
is that where they're given meaning,
or where does the meaning come from?
and when a member of the group asked
if they were on the right path to schlern,
my son shrugged his shoulders,
the tourist walked on and
my son asked:
what did that man want?
did you understand him?

in the restaurant that evening
our pizza margherita tasted extremely good.
by coincidence the german tourists were
in the same establishment and it got very rowdy.
it was so loud that we went up to our room,
we didn't even turn on the tv,

soon fell asleep,
despite the noise from the tavern
floating upstairs.

does a *phoneme* contain a narrative?
a story?
and what about a *grapheme*?
and then:
it all happened twice,
it was all double,
once and then again,
as if to accentuate.
but diplopia
can drive you round the bend,
once you are
aware of it.
there was never just the one tree,
there was always another,
slightly off to the side, slightly above,
while someone burst into tears
full of anger and sheer desperation.
why has god sent us such an abundance
of ways to drown our sorrows
in bottles, in flasks,
to help us in such moments,
to help us over the worst,
to stimulate us to the point of calm again,
for we know,

all will be well again,
as is written in
the handbook of wine connoisseurs.

whenever he was involved
with other people, and he was often
involved with many people,
as we know from neal cassady,
sexual acts were always
part of the proceedings,
just like his grotesque talk,
his wild, associative writing,
even the way he washed his hands,
it was all the same,
which is why his affairs,
which can't be described as such,
never really bothered me.
he always had female acquaintances
and was always out
with girls,
says carolyn cassady in london
on the phone to a journalist
from san francisco.
that's just the way it was,
that's how i see it today.

as soon as i think of my childhood,
i say to a friend one day,

driving through the via carducci
in the fiat in trieste,
i think of hierarchies
in the following way:
preschool: on the ground floor,
elementary school: on the first,
high school: on the second floor,
conference room and CEO
right at the top.

let me repeat:
i don't want to tell a story
the reason for which
is a story in itself.

in our catholic religious education
in my home parish we were taught:
god brought us misery and suffering,
god created disease and famine, because he loved
us so much.
god created our sighs and our melancholy.
god created everything, the heaven, the earth.
this is why it was better not to smile,
or rejoice because you would only have to pay
the price.
god created the pope and the pedophile priests,
god pervades the screams of the wasting and the
wretched,

god cast us into ignis purgatorium,
so we would feel hot and cold,
because he was well-disposed to us.
this is why today i worship the briars and the
stones,
the grass and, above all, the ground,
the earth and the depths of hell,
because i was taught to love god above everything
else.
my god, my god, what have you done to us,
we hear the delirious moaning in hunoldstraße,
innsbruck
and in 57th st in ny.

just a thought to sprinkle over dinner:
how does the phoneme reach us?
and how did it become a grapheme?
was the grapheme modelled around numbers?
or can't you see it like that?
even if you take a scientific approach
toward the whole thing?
just carry on reading
and besides:
it doesn't matter anyway,
as far as the story's concerned.

how are you?
how goes it?

what about
your single kids?
and your lovely wife?
back to the question:
are you talking about my lover?
or my wife?

since when did you stop
smoking?
since my last cigarette.
i know thirst is worse
than homesickness,
as dad always said and
one night i swayed through the town
all on my own
and i knew
i was struggling with seven problems:
monday, tuesday, wednesday etc.

none of that has anything to do with the wind,
i think, and thank you my dear surgeon
from riedering near rosenheim,
thank you for removing an unnecessary growth
from by body,
which for so long
was believed to be
love.

the best form of prevention
against prostate conditions
is jerking off,
old marberger
told his patient
on his rounds.

i miss you so much,
it's hard to get used to the idea
that you're opening your legs
for another man.
but i'm glad, very very glad.

how heavy is the earth?
how vast is my imagination?
how strong is the force
of the wild river tumbling into the valley,
writes slataper in his Karst book
gold feather.

waiter, another drink please,
we shout in purgatory
for our general entertainment.
we also like those
we don't like,
as long as they're good,
says kerschbaumer
amidst the tumultuous applause at the gav

in the old forge,
while schönauer whispers in my ear:
what and who is good,
is known and decided only by others.

if i have to go,
i stay.
if i have to stay,
i go.
that's how easy it is
to get rid of me.

the irredentists really believed
they would be delivered, if their flag flew
over the bay of trieste.
in a tavern there were brawls
and bloody noses
and to calm their nerves
the worried mothers were told
it was all about justice,
you must
put forward your men.
father was proud,
even though he said nothing.

after our separation we would
often bump into each other,
which was a great misfortune,

a man wrote on a piece of paper
in a café in trieste.
i tried to absorb this love,
i was moved to tears
over the knitted sweater,
the wrist watch,
that was supposed to mark a new time,
but we cannot slip
out of time,
so i find myself in trieste
without really knowing
what to do with myself.
the sheet of paper
is folded up and
shoved into a trouser pocket, while
the tourist strolls along the harbor road,
crosses over
and not far from the aquarium
boards the ship to muggia,
where he knows some chess players,
who while away the hours playing
and drinking.
but what happens to the sheet of paper
in the trouser pocket?
a question one could ask
but to which there is no answer.
but one thing's for sure,
no-one will ever see it again.

later the man tells the woman,
for whom he had written those lines,
that it was pleasant,
to be alone, above all, in trieste.

i don't know what father was thinking,
when he brought me into this world,
i sometimes muse,
says an old school friend.
he must've been thinking something,
surely to god,
i ask myself time and again.

we are not of this world.
singing,
shouting,
bawling this line,
we swayed down the bowery
one night,
on our way back to our hotel,
where a handful of night owls
encountered us with friendly smiles,
because they assumed
we were harmless tourists from Europe.

sentences soar into the attics like swallows
reads the motto of an unpublished poetry book.
and behind every successful author

there's an excellent editing office
or so they say on wall street,
as we politely informed
the friendly police officers near a tree
in 454 w. 20th st in new york
in our tyrolean accents.
they obviously had no idea
why we happened to be there
but that's of no consequence.
especially for the guardians of the law.

here's looking at you kid,
says the bored flaneur with the
panama hat on merano promenade.
you know when you're old, my father often said,
when you can see the work to be done
but you're too tired to do it.
how is it that this thought
shoots into his head,
even though he only has eyes for the pretty girl
who has just caught his attention.

oh, how my heart aches,
when i see the bottom of my glass,
sing the patrons from außerfern,
far away from home, devilishly high spirited,
which seems unusual for the alemanns.

language doesn't go through
the mouth – we all know that.
rest gently in the barrage of fire,
walter says to me in the bar.
today red, tomorrow dead,
he adds.

just to stay on topic:
what about copyright?
who has the rights for the potato
and all the letter combinations that go with it,
who owns the math genus?
who does it belong to?
who gets paid for it?
and why?
are we a community
or a pack of individualists?
asks the blasphemer fred in anichstraße.
someone responds:
i've taken the first step
to stop smoking.
i no longer buy cigarettes for myself.
do you mind if i
help myself to yours?

in the german philology department
a new author reads out
a freshly penned text:

the full stop – madness.
the question mark – pure chaos.
not forgetting the paragraphs,
does time have a shore?
where does space implode?
do we only have the past?
where is where?
or in other words:
do we believe in the where,
like we do in the now
that doesn't exist?
or does it?
but where are we now
again?
don't panic,
we have nothing under control,
says a voice over the loudspeaker
in the manicured leisure park.

days later we're sitting in the bixby canyon
near san francisco, a terrifying gorge
with a magical cabin,
in which not only henry miller
penned his *oranges* novel.
but that was several years ago now,
which is why we no longer talk about it,
but sail over to the us one
where at 8pm, on friday 7th october 1955

in fillmore street, san francisco
a sharp new, straight-forward writing –
a remarkable collection of angels
reading on one stage was billed.
philip, mike, allen, gary and another philip
electrify the audience.
the stage in the background,
a drunkard sways with his wine jug,
shouting out go, go, go,
spurring on the poets and the audience,
while we leave the event early
to go for a chinese.
where we see a poster,
referring to today's *charming event*,
with a small passport photo of kenneth rexroth,
who we've just seen,
weeping at the poetry.

the time in tyrol alone
did me the world of good
i went to the seiser alm,
and the schlern,
in glurns,
i took a room in vinschgau.
as you know, i really wanted to go to trieste,
but the storms were raging there,
so i stayed in tyrol.

the communists reduce people
to sausage rolls,
the catholics to the afterlife,
the football coaches to tactics and stamina
for survival on the pitch,
the terrorists to murder and underhanded attacks,
the rebels to a better life on earth,
we learn in the daily paper,
when we start reading between the lines.
but experience tells me
i shouldn't trust the rebels,
who move into the palaces of those they have
overthrown.
just think of the kremlin, just think of castro,
just think of pinochet, shouts michael mcclure
quite beside himself in the café vesuvios in san
francisco,
just round the corner from the city lights book
store.
come on michael, says the rotund
diabetic jack micheline over a beer,
write another song for joplin,
give it to manzarek, so he can sing it
for all eternity.
how right you are, says michael,
who wants to visit gregory corso
in north beach.
but he isn't at home,

he's hanging out
in a few magical bars
with his son max.

by the way i'd like to wish you all
a great weekend,
i hope you all stay respectable
and don't make any kids.
we know the story of the wheat and the chaff,
the adventures of weeds,
the misery of mass murderers.
there comes a time when you have to call a spade a
spade.
but: it's no good,
there's no point.

why are you always so vicious?
are you driven by dark thoughts,
primitive forces?
one word on its own is strange enough.
sentences need a context,
don't they?
entire stories leave those eyes,
winking ambiguously.

on the road in my fiat
in styria.
kernöl und schilcher by r.p. gruber on the back seat,

where the kid's car seats used to be,
in stainz,
past the priory shrouded in fog,
to me it's franz kafka's castle.
at its foot i stroll through
the town and hear:
buy some lottery tickets, your heart will win.
i'm back in my fiat,
thinking of the funnel cake,
i ate at the tavern
run by r.p. gruber's in-laws.
i was sitting under the vine
and as i ate the cake i heard a crack
and my bridge had broken.
which is why i'm traveling with a gap in my teeth
i will never forget
that funnel cake.

i sit in my room, alone.
it's quiet.
no music,
no-one calls.
tomorrow no work,
it's the weekend.
no visits.
no-one's said they're coming.
just in case i hang
a sign on the door:

i'm here, but i'm not.
it's quiet
and i feel i'm in heaven.

ah, america, i don't know you.
i've only visited you a few times.
you are rich and equally as dumb and
you have had glorious days,
but you brought the mushroom into this world.
your guilt is as endless
as route 66 is long,
the 66
always pops into my mind,
with all the crazy folks,
back, far back in the rockies,
where the dreamers can sing kaddish all day long,
but one day
america, you will have to change your ways,
even though i'm here just as a tourist,
just to have some fun,
on my way through minnesota toward duluth
to hibbing high school and back to sturgeon lake,
where years earlier i taught
a hoard of kids to canoe,
then on the greyhound to minneapolis,
to see corso lying in his daughter's apartment
on his death bed.

what should i do?
which way do i turn?
after all, there are children involved.
why can't i cope.
these are the sentences,
that will tide me over
again this week.
small steps to begin with:
go to bed early,
eat regularly.
don't lose contact with the outside world.
and to sum up:
it could work, but it won't.
i could but i can't.
i'd like to but i won't.

although it all happened such a long time ago
it will never let him go
it will stay with him till the day he dies
one day this line appeared in a short story
and caused quite a stir,
because it was written
without a comma and without a full stop
no capital letters
not pleasing on the eye.
this may not have been anything new,
but some thought it unusual,
especially for those who knew

the man who
has since passed away.

so many people before me
have survived death
and so that it makes me think
i might survive it too,
my deceased father always used to say
usually on quiet saturday afternoons,
while listening to the request show
with margit humer-seeber
and the song
heimat deine sterne,
which moved my father to tears,
consumed
by the memory
of his time as a prisoner of war in russia,
when the russians on an icy cold christmas night,
played the song over a loudspeaker,
to break them once and for all.
the whole camp cried,
it said in the family book,
but in all those years
back at home
the song
never
sounded as moving
as it did

then
in russia
as a prisoner,
father always said.

what was that story
you told?
did we hear you right?
or is it you just spinning one of your yarns?
about something you cobbled together from a time
that never existed for us?
nonsense! was the answer,
it still doesn't really matter.
just don't trust your ears
or your eyes.
god only knows
what happened there.

reuters has released an exclusive report,
we heard on the radio,
about a japanese company
buying up the german alphabet.
apparently, the deal is worth millions.
the association of authors has protested, saying
you can't treat language like a commodity.
oh, and what language will they
use in the sales contract?
that is still under negotiation, they say.

at any rate, the writers have
threatened to stop writing,
if the letters of the alphabet really do
fall into japanese hands,
they will boycott the alphabet,
the bulletin states.
at the conference
working groups
planned a series of counter measures
including a completely new alphabet,
to escape the stranglehold
of the japanese multinational.

the separation he was told he'd never get over,
opened his eyes
to many beautiful things.
the hardest thing was that
it was as if it were happening every day.
it wasn't until his wife's lover
put a gun to his head
at midnight
in an alleyway
near the hospital
that this separation became more exciting.
this event was actually
the only thing that made him happy,
that he was proud of,
even though he'd never told a soul.

because no-one had wanted to listen.
one thing's for sure,
there are loads of good stories out there
but not many good listeners
and what's the point of a good story
if it disappears in a puff of smoke
in a forest
among birdsong,
as romantic as this
thought may be.
but as i was saying
there are too few listeners
to a good story.
and i'm one of them.

destroy me, annihilate me;
but don't leave me alone,
gianni sighed in trieste,
when he and his brother
volunteered to go to war with the irridentists,
to fight for a new homeland.
which the brother never saw,
gianni, on the other hand, died an old man
which he saw as an evil twist of
fate.
no, no, it can't be
that so much pain in this world is for nothing,
he had once wanted to write

on a slip of paper for his mother,
before descending from the opicina into town,
past the lighthouse,
where he bumped into
the young poet serra on the street.
serra once wrote in a poem:
when war comes, he will come too,
when the time is ripe,
for man does not
make history.
as the two greeted each other
serra ran his fingers through his hair,
then they went their separate ways.
soon after serra fell near podgora
hit by enemy fire
and gianni returned to isonzo.

run, says the soccer coach,
run for all you're worth.
that's the austrian tactic
as our national team
once again
suffers a glorious defeat.
but you can't wallow in your problems
day in day out, says the concrete cutter
at the bar
after the game,
after all, we're austrians

and well used to defeat
and anyway i'm set up for a great night
with one of my lovers.
six months later he buys himself a new work car,
with the advertising slogan:
a man and his saw fight for survival!

if you don't go with the times,
says our boss,
you will go with time.
as always
i feel uncomfortable in my own skin,
even if the statistics tell us
that the average driver
spends three years of his life
in traffic.
the church, a voice says in the back alley,
has a strong stomach,
and since his hemorrhoid operation,
if nothing else,
at least he's a healthy asshole.

i weigh one hundred and ten kilos,
therefore i am.
things aren't like they used to be though.
the weekends
when we would charge into town
and dance the fertilization dance,

are now well in the past.
just like the days
when the day began at nightfall.

no one leaves the room without moving,
shouts hubert in his cowboy hat at the tiger inn
to all the regulars,
his pop gun drawn and
the friendly smile of the world in his face.
a man stands at home at the front door
holding his hat and briefcase,
wondering
if he's just come home from work
or is just going.
he can't decide.

there are more cranks in the world than chinese
it says in the encyclopedia.
relationships only damage those
who don't have any,
it is said.
since owning a cell phone,
i always feel
like i'm carrying a payphone round with me.
waiter, another round please, we've been saying for days.
apropos: are we already at war
or just in the casino?
a bewildered corporal asks.

when i'm at innsbruck christmas market,
i'd rather be at the one in bolzano,
and when i'm standing at the
mulled wine bar in merano,
i picture myself in
the city of mozart.
why is that?
someone asks
whilst wondering whether
he should look up a shrink
to shed light on his childhood.

table dances are cheaper in the four roses,
but your neighbor watches on from the next table
and gets his pleasure that way.
in the new snake no one watches on,
you're just not allowed to touch them, the women,
that is.
but you can't do that in the four roses either
say the housewives at the bébé
over a prosecco in the evening.

husbands are for money
and the backdoor man is for love,
chuckle emancipated women in the coffee house
one morning.
heinz's resistance is of another kind.
fascism can only be fought with turbo fascism.

money with even more money.
madness with even more madness.
cars with even more cars.
and if you own a house,
the others should get five more
rows of houses,
whole districts,
whole landscapes filled with houses
without relenting.
this is the only way resistance works,
says heinz knowingly.

owning nothing just like hc artmann
and being courted
like a baroque poet
suffices.
that's all you need,
because i don't understand
anything more about life
anyway.

how are you?
how was your night?
are you out?
when will we see
each other again?
i miss you.
i'm thinking of you.

at last i can write to you again,
though i don't know where you are.
oh god, why did it have to be this way?
i was walking at twilight
wondering where you would be right now.
for a moment i felt sure
death isn't real.
i really hoped
we'd share many more years together.
i miss you,
you are still within me.
when will you finally leave me,
when will you disappear from my life?

are we the imperfect part of god?
are we all that is evil, the scum of the earth?
are we the mistake in perfection
or in other words:
are we the fools of this whole divine
business?
what do you think?
i'm just saying.
i don't expect an answer.
sometimes it's good
to keep quiet.

is the universe one big cinema screen,
showing our flickering lives,

so that the lord our father
can amuse himself by watching our clips
for his own entertainment,
to pass the time of day?
my head is a confusion of thoughts,
as i stumble out of the bebe
into museumstraße
and start moving toward the tax office
via marktgraben.
there i find the bus stop, mulling over
the barkeeper's parting words.
i can't work them out.
but it's late
and there are so many things
mortal man doesn't understand.

what can i get you?
a large or a small beer?
a small beer please,
a small one is big enough today.

why, i ask myself,
are sentences ignored?
don't they have their own raison d'etre?
do they just mumble on?
i start thinking,
while in trieste
taking the boat

to muggia.
i know a former boxer there,
who always has
good beer in the fridge,
and a whole host of better stories.

now it's official
i announce
on a red park bench:
i don't want to meet any more sentences,
especially not those
that march in at the top of their voices.
i no longer need a bauhaus
and can do without bookshelves.

and anyway:
what sentences should i use
to get me through the week?
why don't the ones i have
seem to be enough?
why don't they seem adequate?
why is talking to people
such an effort?
is it because of my strong medication?

the following sentence
was sprayed in red paint
onto the wall of a house

in the city center:
wealth requires poverty.......
early one evening in february
i happen upon it
and am baffled by the seven dots
added on the end.
it's one of those wonderful moments,
when the streets are dusty,
and everything's bathed in a pleasant blue light.
what's this claim all about?
i find myself asking.
is someone trying to seem important?
what are comments like this about?
and more than that:
what do we do with them?
when the machine's running smoothly,
it spews it all out:
who, in heaven's name, put it there?
did they want passers-by
to feel guilty?
and then there's the question,
the question of the seven dots
sprayed at the end of the sentence.
are the dots the point of interest,
the clever part of this assertion?
what was the sprayer thinking
when spraying on the dots?
are they a provocation?

a question mark?
an insight?
was he trying to put wealth and poverty
into perspective?

whose wealth? whose poverty?
wasn't he just talking about material things,
material wealth, material poverty?
do the dots allow the interpretation
that humankind
wouldn't actually be happier,
if everyone had a full belly
and a roof over their heads?
was the sprayer thinking about that?
is such a sentence the sputum of a simple mind,
a begrudger,
someone who feels short changed,
a wannabe-agitator,
or a rebel,
a revolutionary,
a do-gooder,
the idea of an idiot?
what's a sentence like that about?
grumbles a pensioner
with a billa shopping bag
in her right hand.

later in a small tavern
two friends talk about the spray paint,
especially about the seven dots
at the end.
they're puzzling over their meaning,
while drinking white wine spritzers
as night gradually falls.
one of them runs his thumb
and index finger over his moustache and says,
the sprayer's statement
would remind me of a washing powder ad
if it wasn't for those dots,
that were disposed to
blurring any previous clarity.
late at night
they start discussing
more questions:
is this statement justified?
where will it lead?
is it a distraction?
what conclusions should be drawn?
is it all pointless?

do we have to face up to it?
is it an impermissible simplification?
doesn't it just appeal to nothing more
than the dark, inferior instincts
of humankind?

is it, as a consequence, indirectly
telling us
to allow all hell to break loose?
should the sprayer
be called to account
for causing a civil nuisance?
would the world be a better place
if this statement were never made?
questions asked years ago
night after night
in the artists café,
that no longer exists
after the married owners
filed for bankruptcy.
but still the question remains
what prompted the sprayer
to add
exactly seven dots to the sentence.......
exactly seven dots, just like the ones
noted in a red notebook many years ago.
the notebook was rediscovered quite by accident
and the finder scratched his head in bewilderment,
as he looked at the writing.

i've been working hard on becoming mentally infirm
as has been medically confirmed.
though not officially.
but rest assured we'll get there.

after all: who are we.
even if we're told
from above
that we don't live *off* art,
but *for* art.
it may seem far-fetched but art production
comes from having to and wanting to.
also
since our childhood we have
tried our utmost to keep away from work
and to make way for everyone else.
but one more thing: i've been stuck
inside myself for days.
what do you think?
apart from the mental infirmity i mentioned.
how can anyone keep it together
twenty-four hours a day?
sometimes our strength fails us.
and all we can do is escape into the past,
our memories.
talking of garlic.
it's unbelievable.
i understand
a beautiful person can't be disfigured,
even if he can't decide
what to wear today.
but there are other days too.

perhaps my confusion,
the depiction of my confusion,
is all because of my eyes.
it certainly can't be entirely
ruled out, considering how long
i've been struggling with it.
it's the rapid fatigue,
you see, because of the extra image
i have to suppress
to get through each day.

believe me,
i don't expect thanks
or trouble either.
we just cling onto the hope
that everything will get better.
health is everything.
hence the garlic,
fat-free food and no candy.
we're just a little less disciplined
with the liquid.
everyone needs
something to live for,
and something to die for.

humor is when laughing sticks in your throat.
in maria alm someone
threw himself in the water, suicide.

he failed, as he was saved.
so he tried again three days later
with a noose.
this time it worked.
in maria alm they say:
he hung himself up to dry.
his laundry, now a problem of the past
never to bother him again.
just saying, cos we were talking about humor.

at least your double vision means
that both halves of your brain are working,
someone says one day,
who, meaning well, tried to
understand this phenomenon.
this affliction also
conceals the advantage,
looking at it positively,
that you can see both sides
right from the start,
giving you your own rounded view on things.

it's true
that not every biro,
pencil or fine-liner is suited to writing,
someone says at a literary talk
one weekend.
that novel i wrote was a flop,

richard brautigan said one evening
at the café trieste in san francisco,
because i wrote my notes
in blue ink.
but i had nothing else to hand
on this god-forsaken farm in montana
and as i wrote the first few lines
i came to terms with the knowledge
that it was going to be a flop.
but i just couldn't be bothered
to look out for another pen
so i just carried on writing,
brautigan continued,
whilst polishing his smith & wesson in the backyard.

days after in trieste
corso said to him:
a writing utensil is a balancing act
and if you don't know that
you know nothing about writing,
nothing about poetry,
nothing about the color and melody of words.

leaving home, corso says,
with my son max
to play pool at haight ashbury,
walking into the city lights,
i see no alternative

than to raid the city light book store
of lawrence ferlinghetti
and to use the spoils
to buy two flights,
flights for a trip to new york,
as i couldn't stomach the drive
on route 66 in my vw bus.

in the early hours of the morning
carrying his son max on his shoulders,
corso pays his respects
to brautigan
and on his way to his vw bus,
in which they sleep,
gregory thinks of shelley
and thinks of keats
and of the protestant cemetery
near campo de fiori in rome.
he's the only one missing now;
just a question of time
until his ash and his glory
find their way there.

when you're down,
you can fall no further,
says the family history book,
or: god, give everyone who knows me
ten times more than they'd like me to have,

or: give flowers while they're living,
for on graves they're just a waste.
all this is written.

we have no money,
my forefathers used to say,
when after months of absence
they returned from the construction sites in swabia.
though we have brought no money with us,
we have plenty of new songs
to see us through the winter.
then it all happened so fast:
boozing without drinking,
guzzling without eating,
fucking without sex,
sailing round the world
without moving from the spot,
and if nothing else works,
we'll leave everything behind.

i spoil all my lovers
to excess, says regina.
i can't bear having a cold stone
lying next to me in bed.
when a man wants love,
i send him out into the night,
only letting him by my side
hours later,

once he has returned to his senses
and has got rid of any fluffy thoughts.
between the sheets, i want neither vulgarity nor love,
just good sex.
just so you know.
we're sitting on the patio,
cigarette smoke floating into the air,
she crosses her slender legs,
and wraps her knitted cardigan more tightly
around her body.

kerouac, i later say to myself,
you destroyed yourself,
i didn't find the stupid comments
you made in your TV interviews embarrassing,
nixon and vietnam, my ass ...
i want to stand by you even after so many years,
they should've left you in peace:
less whisky
less port
less beer
be it in northport
orlando
lowell
or even
jacksonville, florida.
just so you know
we're on the same wavelength.

we didn't need freud to tell us
it gets louder above
when it goes quiet below.
and pay your dues,
so you don't need to be ever grateful.
and:
i've never been indebted
to anyone.
it's sentences like these that we have to endure.
the phoneme and the grapheme
haven't passed anyone's lips.
and while we're on the topic:
who do we hold the mirror to?
who do we provoke?
who do we get thinking?
could anything be more ridiculous
from the artist's point of view?

just so you know
how to take this letter,
a friend is told
who was upset that
his buddy hadn't written for so long.
the answer was clear.

it may be naïve – but where
do letters find their content?
for example: they used to say,

when the kids have flown the nest
and her husband's six feet under,
a woman's life can finally start.
or during the saturday night western, they would say:
shoot a flaming arrow in
that scumbag's wooden leg.
or the headline: man plans murder
and buys axe at hardware store.
or: indian drums up troops.
or at the end: he died quite suddenly.

at any rate letters are made of flesh and blood.
but: how do they get inside?
how do they find their way in?
who mixes the sound?
who bears the responsibility?
what have they got to do with me?
which letters are mine?
who has the copyright on them?
and:
how is a letter born?

from the world of politics we know
the baby that screams loudest
is always the first to have its diaper changed.

franz and i sit in his workshop,
the log burner kicking out plenty of heat,

it's christmas.
we down a few metronios and eisenwurz,
and his son says:
ah, there you sit, you old timers,
telling each other christmas stories
from the seventies.
if god
imagined us
then he should have us,
as we are,
i think,
getting up
and trudging through the snow to the service plaza,
to celebrate christmas eve.

the church is a business without any goods,
represented by the divine ground staff,
the best business concept for the past two thousand
years.
what a great idea to use salvation and damnation
as a marketing strategy!
such thoughts spring to mind
around christmas
when franz is on fire,
at midday on christmas eve,
drinking fire-water by the log burner in his workshop.

is handke a writing maniac, as robert says,
or bernhard an author,
who always writes
about the same topics,
without taking any risks,
and, donning his lederhosen, never contemplated
failure,
as franz from winterthur claims?
is jelinek a worthy nobel prize winner,
whose texts are nigh on impossible
to read, like karl says in leifers?
brecht always dropped his pants,
to service the women,
as marcel reich-ranicki of all people
once claimed on a talkshow.
did joyce really fall off his chair
every day in trieste
lying on the floor next to his empty crate of beer,
as they say?
what's it all supposed to mean?
how do we take it in?
how do we deal with it?

ever since i became impotent,
i've really started getting along with women,
it is said.
never give in,
but sprinkle in a little more gunpowder

to escalate the situation,
someone scribbled on a loose sheet of paper.
do letters sound like
rusty bicycle chains,
or:
like ringing syllable forks,
which the jury member
at the bachmann prize-giving
misread as silver forks,
and criticized the word choice,
whereupon the cigarette smoke got stuck in her throat
and robert schindel's jaw dropped.

i write the way i write not
for an audience.
why does he do it anyway?
why does he seek publicity?
aren't the best poets
the unpublished ones, not because
they were rejected,
but because they remained within their own four
walls,
and never sought a public stage?

when my friend franz
visits me from the neighboring village,
i'm sometimes overcome with this feeling
that he's just alighted from a flying object,

everything seems so detached, so far away,
distant, the language,
which for months we often couldn't understand.
lit up,
his youthful face glows,
flashes of light shooting through his head,
overwhelming me with wonder and amazement.
he must be from a different star.

when i look into my apartment
i'm surprised.

i only asked him what he did for a living,
i hear someone say, aghast,
and i try to calm him down
cos that's the kind of guy i am.
no more silly questions,
i say, he's a medium,
from outer space,
he shoots down in his ufo,
and in his hands, matter seeks its form.
that's it,
a task.
nothing to do with
a profession.
and certainly nothing to do
with being a *sculptor*.

always this fear
of falling short of expectations.

when it comes to writing, franz taught me
that every a4 sheet of paper is different:
for hours we discussed margins,
rambling on and on about the spaces between the
lines
about the broken white of the paper,
talking for days
scrutinizing closely
the weight of each sheet.
we spent months pondering
the brightness and darkness of letters
and the shiny faces of a4 sheets.

we share our experiences
every hour
we spend together.
not to mention the melody of each syllable
or those letters
that require so much effort
they send us to distraction.
but it always brings us a step further forward.
because that's the whole point,
as we realized from the very first moment
we met,
and since learning from him

i've lost my innocence and naivety
in my use of paper,
it was only through him
that i became a serious writer,
as is apparent
from the notes
of an egomaniac.

per teletext i learn of something
completely different.
just no more men,
because i can't deal
with that anymore,
says a woman
i've been in love with for so long.
not even a one-night stand
at a far-away address
and certainly no subsequent phone calls,
at best a
hidden smile at the thought
of the goodnight kiss
in the early hours behind the door,
that no-one must see,
but that's so long ago.

max, an old friend of a friend
from a far-away village
has died.

a wonderful man,
says my friend.
he never realized
what beautiful things he'd created.
he never noticed.
he was never interested.
all just passing fads,
said max,
with all due respect.
his hands oozed work,
all those years those hands
had followed a cause.
do you understand, says my friend
and for a moment
we feel very close before he climbs
back inside his flying machine
and takes off,
over the river,
over the flood plains,
over the alder trees and bushes
the river landscape,
before his ghost
disappears
within his own four walls.

he owned a car that
was made entirely of spare parts.
max was insulted

that he couldn't get
a tollway permit sticker for it.
that broke his heart.
he couldn't understand it
and he supposed
they weren't just playing a dirty trick on him
no, they wanted to get rid of him for good.
a few days later he died.

every word is a truth,
every sentence a philosophy
and outside the heat is unbearable.
time passes,
summer will soon be over,
as will the autumn and winter, and
the spring as well,
who cares,
can i have the check please,
i want to go home
and watch TV.

yes... i'm feeling wistful and
melancholy
yes... there are days when
i ooze self-pity,
i long for the peace
that follows death,
the poet from the café central

writes in a letter to me from the madhouse.
he's gained 30 pounds in weight
because of the medication,
all he wants is to die
because he'll never regain
his former weight.

somehow i lost sight of the poet
from the café central,
even though i never quite forgot him.
in recent years i haven't
been out much, so i rarely
frequented the central.
even the poet from the café central
wasn't seen there very often
before being admitted to the madhouse.
anyway, i think i'll go and visit him soon
at the sanatorium in hall,
even though we don't have much to say.

life has become
so overwhelming,
i always feel
it has numbed me,
i read on a postcard
the poet from the café central
had sent me
several years ago from big sur.

that was the last i heard of him,
we lost sight of each other after that.

where do we come from?
where are we going?
why are we here?
what's it all about?
these are the questions
to which none
of the answers
fit.

by the way: i'm here,
but not here,
says the note still hanging on my front door.
no such thing as good and evil.
just like the force of gravity isn't a force,
as einstein taught us,
even though without resistance
we all fall at the same speed,
wherever we fall.
be it up
or down.
the smaller the dick,
says my buddy,
the racier the cars.
it's a sunny saturday morning.
we're in merano

under the arbors
the waiters are clearing the tables to one side
as a convoy of wailing lamourghinis squeezes
past.

praise chemistry
and all its offshoots,
the pharma industry
and all its products
someone sings
somewhere
all alone
a song of praise to pills,
tablets,
prescriptions,
medication,
that have given me life
over the past thirty-five years
helping me get through each day.
the constant fatigue
the depressing corpulence
made my life harder,
but i live.
the refrain begins again
at this late or early hour,
depending on how you see it.
the neighbors wonder
the next day

what in god's name
was going on in here last night.

the writing computer produces an abundance of texts;
no writing inhibitions built into the program.
but there are days when the selection is hard to make,
the mood disharmonious.
when you lose your touch,
you can always go and do something else for a while.
written on the screen, it says:
globalization leads to rise of nationalism,
and if something's going to plan
then it's my irregular sex life.

since i found out
that helmut was an altar boy
in the parish church in his youth
i understand the way he writes,
i say to fuchs, the artist, at leipziger platz,
whereupon fuchs puts a schnapps glass to his lips
and i'm no longer sure
if i got through to him.

what bugs me about jesus is the disciples
but it's no real use.
they say:
keep going
and:

keep your chin up.
regina says teasingly:
when judging a man
only three things count for women:
length, stability and endurance.
of course, she watches far too many soaps.
she thinks highly of men,
so long as they're on time,
take care of themselves
and never stay all night.
she can't abide wandering hands in the night.
over breakfast
she prefers to gaze out of the window
than into the eyes of last night's lover.

it's possible,
but it's not,
i could,
but i can't,
i should
but why should i.
answers over answers.

i was at gare de l'est last fall
a tin can like the one in radkersburg,
where i appeared
as a steaming polenta dish.
these are sentences i took

from the papers of the café central poet
when visiting him in hospital,
while caught in the following conversation:
why, i ask, are sentences ignored?
don't they have their own lives?
do they just muddle through?
the question is asked,
while my thoughts drift to trieste
where i take the boat
to muggia,
because i know a retired boxer there,
who always has a stash of
good beer in the fridge,
and tells the best stories.

always this brutal change of location,
from here to there.

during the crossing
the conversation
is all about the I in kafka
and in nietzsche.
letters are patient.
what do words think?
what do sentences think?
we letters insist on our meaning!

you get out of a pig,
what you put into it:
i'm talking about the meat
of a wiener schnitzel.
gambling debts and election promises
are not enforceable
say the hemp brothers
in the pergola at the sports ground.

is white everything or nothing?
and how is that meant?
is white supposed to be nothing
or
is white supposed to be everything?
i need a holiday
inside myself
peace and tranquility away from myself,
this sentence suddenly pops up
on a 1970s postcard
of clemens-hofbauer square
in the 17th district of vienna.
today, it's difficult to know
what to make of it,
because youth has faded.
and he hanged himself with a hemp noose,
a short story begins, after misunderstanding
the question of whether he had a thing for hemp.
rock lives, there's no question,

and not just since
he was hit by a rock
which dealt him a deadly blow to the head.

the stock exchange is a legalized crime scene,
says a confused man embroiled in a discussion
that doesn't really interest him,
just like economic growth
and the unemployment rate,
even though they all affect him, more or less.
at munich airport, a few elderly gentlemen
were waiting for friends from vancouver,
the news about the iraq war
was showing on ntv,
while the share prices
hurried across the bottom of the screen
from left to right,
and the canadian visitor said
so much honesty exists only in the west.

the general's widow, far beyond eighty,
with a powdered face,
black penciled eyebrows,
a true lady, would order a taxi every other week.
the chauffeur already knew the run well.
they'd cruise along the interstate for around 38 miles,
their destination a well-established brothel,
which high officers

often frequented
during the war.
the general's widow always
had her demented fifty-year-old son
in tow, the porter would take the son indoors,
the lady waited outside
until the porter escorted the son back to the car.
she settled the bill for the love service
that was due to her son every other week.
he never got close to a woman on his own,
so she had to arrange it for him.
this gave her life a little meaning,
but what would become of him
if she were no longer alive?

don't you understand, they bawl at the confused
man,
if you buy shares, you haven't understood what
life's about.
although the confused man had lucid moments,
he didn't know what to make of shares and stock
exchanges
and the unemployed anymore,
even though in younger years he had written
socially critical articles for the *zukunft* in vienna.
this was all in the past now
and he probably didn't do it from the bottom of his
heart even then

for he felt he had a different vocation
in life.
but what was it now?
he couldn't find the answer.
he wasn't exactly in a good place
as he left the building in argentinierstraße.
but he does have better days,
hovering like a ray of light above him.
surely, that can't have been it,
he thought,
as the seven dots
sprayed on the wall
float into his mind.

the authoress threw the beginning of the story
about the old general's wife
and her demented son
into the trash
and decided
she had been reading
too much márquez recently.
she needed to return to her roots.
now and then south american finger exercises
aren't a bad idea.
after all, you can't think about work all the time.

if you don't want progress,
stand down!

if you're not roman catholic,
don't take
catholic public holidays!
during my stint as arbitrator
no-one can go bankrupt.
that was the credo of a relative,
after taking over as branch manager
of raiffeisen bank.
help those who are worse off than yourself,
then you'll never be out of work.
he was too unmusical for the music band
and too fiery for the fire department.
so he became an author,
and he too, had his credo:
when writing,
you have to catch the right moment:
not too early
not too late.
when the time's right
the short stories will flow.
in his surroundings they even appreciate him
here and there.

commuting at lightning speed between
vienna, trieste, rome, lowell, jacksonville and zirl
back and forth,
is a pilgrimage of a special kind.
i sit in an overheated room

unable to explain
where all the heat is coming from.
in kals they're all drunk,
it apparently said on the computer.
the question remains,
whether the machine was switched on
at the right time,
at the right point in time.

at the chamber of commerce, they say
you have to buy in everything.
actually it's time
i threw myself into the arms of a lady of the night,
the artist thinks to himself.
he's well into his eighties
and merciless.
the massive body with a glass in hand
props up the bar
and follows the dancer on the little stage.
you can always do better.
why is everyone in kals drunk?
why are they always drunk?
why?
why in kals of all places?

childhood memories in rome
not far from campo der fiori,
where the urn

containing gregory corsos' ashes
now lies.

the double vision of my youth:
you're so lucky,
they would say,
because when you have ten schillings
in your hand,
you actually think you have twenty.
enough about that.
anyway, we used to say
that all the adults
in our street
had wallets
made of onion leather
because whenever they peered inside,
they'd start crying.
at the cemetery in rome,
i find myself standing in front of three graves
wondering what else i
should do while i'm here.

just don't
say a word to anyone,
not a word,
don't give anything away,
his old friend
told him

late one night.
don't meet anyone,
or bump into anyone.
don't say a word,
no conversation,
don't look for a chat,
you're no longer intellectual enough for that.
don't share your suffering
with anyone,
only your happiness.
in trieste of all places
it came as a complete surprise,
there of all places,
in the jewish quarter
and later
in san marco,
where he, far at the back,
near the restrooms,
took a seat and
glanced across
to a very old woman,
who he knew well from heresay,
with whom he had often wanted to talk;
just not now, no... not now,
nothing in this world
would make him want to
talk
to this fascinating person just now.

you can't take on too much.
sometimes it's important
to know your station,
and stay within your limits.

searching for oneself,
needing an anchor
in trieste,
as the world falls apart.
a haircut during working hours.
he was a businessman,
and as a buyer
you'd worry he wasn't charging enough.
he was fond of his customers
and his path to insolvency
forseeable.
but let's hope for the best,
even though we all know
how it will end.
but:
he's still in the thick of it,
and:
it hasn't happened yet,
and:
he still has hope.

having such dazzling good looks as mine,
is something women find difficult to bear.

so in recent years
i preferred to stay single.
several times in my life,
my mind has been broken into,
it has been plundered and robbed,
but never reported to the police.
every sentence an attack,
every word a bullseye,
every syllable a cutting tone,
every letter the right sign.
phonemes and graphemes – a rebellion.
phoneme and grapheme lying in each other's arms
like a couple of young lovers
after a wild night between the sheets,
filled with feelings of happiness.
there are days
so different to those in san marco,
when the old lady
gave the man, lost for words,
a friendly glance
on her way to the bathroom.

at first he was the only owner of a cell phone,
a personal payphone at the table in the tavern,
someone had said on the train to vienna,
but then it wasn't long before
everyone at the table in the tavern
was a cell phone user.

one day it got to the point where
one personal payphone
at the table in the tavern
called
another personal payphone
at the table in the tavern.
the table in the tavern had become
a communication bunker.

we speak faster now
because of the phone charges.

his psychological illness
that went back to his childhood
kept him and his family under a spell.
at home everyone spoke in a whisper,
every noise was avoided, visits banned
but when it became unbearable,
he went to the doctor's and concluded,
he really didn't feel that bad.
as a result of his illness, he said,
his life had taken on a quality of its own,
as everyone around him agreed.
he was an artist, he said, and would usually lie
on the bench by the stove.
his self-image was defined by
his rejection of everything
created in the past two hundred years,

which doesn't mean,
that everything before then was worth seeing.
details fascinated him:
the concealed,
the hidden,
the overlooked,
lying around for centuries unnoticed.
he never allowed his photo to be taken,
because no photo produced an adequate reflection
of his being.
he denied the art world:
too ridiculous,
too modern,
too pompous.
when he was invited
to present one of his works
to an audience of art lovers,
he lowered a head-high block of granite
into a hole in the ground and covered it with
earth
and he told the people there,
that they were standing on a buried work of art.
from this day onward
his eccentricity was
lauded in the art world.
later it was revealed
he had exhibited sculptures
in a new york gallery,

and had covered them
with hand-woven cloth.

it deeply impressed art circles even in new york.
i won't accept the criticism
that it's jumbled chaos.
it's just that it's not clearly structured.
the response of the audience in new york
angered him no end,
i add this
just to pick up on what was said before.
no-one took any notice of the covering up,
no-one cared about the hand-woven cloth,
the artist cussed.
but what else do you expect in new york,
and of the new yorkers.
it's all so yesterday
even before it's been created.
and it was our artist,
thoroughly caught up in rural tradition,
who took
the rock
that killed the confused man
and concealed it in a covered display case
in his studio.
just like the caps from the beer bottles
they had emptied at their last meeting
on christmas eve.

he himself never downed more than two bottles of beer
and only did so to please his friend.

if syntax continues to be used in the same way,
nothing much will ever change.
life is a cut up, noted william burroughs one day
in the parisian beat hotel in git le coeur
in the presence of brian gysin in the nineteen fifties.
or, to quote voghera from trieste:
we can't survive as socialists and
capitalists,
if that's our intention.
every sentence fights against it.
even in the holy scriptures we read
that humanity can only survive
in a community formed through necessity.
giorgio voghera had heard this in his early years,
we can say today with great certainty.
and bill burroughs still insists: life is a cut up.

i would like a husband,
says regina, while i sit
next to her feeling contrite,
a husband who fulfils my every
wish and otherwise leaves me alone.
waldrapps are circling overhead
threatened by extinction.

never trust people who
can understand poems,
paul bowles once told me in tangier,
only bad poems can be understood,
never the good ones.
he closed his eyes
allowing himself a quick cat nap
in his rocking chair.
he awoke,
i said goodbye,
starting to leave.
with a great effort paul stood up,
and his friend escorted him to his bedroom.

and so he may fall,
the visitor starts to think,
all that hot air,
and the afternoons with burroughs,
donning thin linen suits,
neckties and grey linen hats
from the twenties,
like two cia agents
sitting in bars and staring
outside with disgust on their faces
looking for cool guys
as they say in lowell at the kerouac festival
in merrimack street.

i'm convinced,
says a friend,
with a vehemence and force
i've never seen in him before
that death is like one incredible orgasm.
at any rate:
it'll be interesting to find out
though i don't need to know for a while yet,
i still feel good
and am happy with my
unspectacular orgasms.

later they're sitting in a café
drinking apple juice with pesticide and a small coffee
and they ask the waitress
how her orgasms are.
she says she can't complain just now,
her private parts are well perfused,
no cause for concern,
she admits quite openly
before the conversation takes a serious turn:
he says, he thinks about death every day,
he just can't help it.
then they leave,
the evening draws to an end.
how much do we owe?
how much is still due?
all paid.

everybody goes home in october,
plays david amram
and his trio in a bar in the bowery,
where he performed way back
in the fifties.
jack wrote his books with his life,
says the literature student and guide
leading a literary tourist group.
they stroll along the shores of the merrimack,
lined on both banks by old factory buildings,
where jack's mother once earned her living.

whatever:
i prefer stories to reality.
FOREIGNERS GO HOME!
some young twerp sprays
on a wall in vienna.

the customer is king,
sing the sales assistants from
the euro-spar store,
donning red-green skirts
at the christmas party,
but the pope,
we don't serve people
who think they're the pope.
the honorary councilor of commerce applauds
the tuneful company choir at the sillpark mall

where late at night a checkout girl says,
she's perfectly happy with her figure,
especially considering her age,
at thirty-seven, she says, you can't expect
to have the butt of an eighteen year old,
that's just the way it is and anyway,
she says slightly tipsy,
as a checkout girl and human being
she's certainly dumb enough to get through life.
but the councilor of commerce doesn't
hear.

yesterday the barcardi-connection
was back again,
the barman complains.
five in the morning, the birds were singing,
and all because the clowns from the alpine trio
could't bring themselves to leave.
but nothing's quite like life itself,
he moans, his face an angry red.

to be a good writer
you have to peddle with your life
and use it for that purpose,
says bob kaufmann
at the jack-kerouac school
in boulder colorado.
that at least is what ann waldman

christian ide hintze and christan loidl
said at the airport in schwechat.
but let's just flash back.
the task of literature
is not to perceive other people
as hydrants with no feelings,
max brod said to martin buber
in a café in wroclaw.
could you please stay on topic?
they call out
from the control desk onto the stage.

it's a wonderful day in early october
at nickeys, in gorham street, lowell.
curls of smoke hanging in the air,
dissolving into thin threads,
waiting for jack,
who comes in drunk,
bag of whiskey in hand,
broke as always.
intermittently, he and his bag
disappear into the bathroom,
because regular drinks don't
fire him up,
in lowell,
northport, jacksonville,
or orlando florida,
and after every short

visit to the bathroom,
he returns a little more tipsy.

is god a personal god who looks after
each and every one of us individually?
asks kerouac.
jack disappears into the bathroom again
with his bag,
while the bar owner
gives him forgiving looks.
are we fallen angels?,
shouts jack into one of the player's faces
thrusting the cue into the felt,
ripping it.
he bawls into the half-filled bar:
heaven is glorious,
but it should be here for us as well.
why must we face the madness of time,
the unbearable certainty of death.
why? what for?
shouts jack in his whiskey voice,
as he clambers around the pool table
in nickey's bar,
cue in hand.

many years later,
long after jack's death
every year

in july
someone here at nickey's
reads from his big-sur text.

in all religions god is the term
for the other, the completely other.

poverty isn't shameful
it says in my calendar.
so what about wealth?
another such question.
well, i'd rather be sad
and depressed in a mercedes
than in a packed streetcar,
says my old friend.
misery has a name:
budweiser!
the days
when we would talk about
poverty and wealth
through the night
are long gone,
as you can read
here.

desperate, i
destroyed my cell phone.
there it lay on the floor

shattered in a thousand pieces,
i took a picture of it.

i've often been very lucky in my lifetime,
i've met plenty of wonderful people
who've shown me great kindness.
is it enough to live for the day
and sleep through the night?

you have to say it over and over,
repeat it over and over:
if you bring murderers,
warlords, bums,
or professional footballers into your home
you have to expect the worst,
or so it says in the latest issue of the parish magazine.

the bowels are emptied once a day,
in the morning before work,
say the comics at the chamber of commerce.
anyway it's my birthday today,
so that's it for another year,
as an art card floats into my mailbox
in august.

oh, how bad would it be,
if we had television interviews
with franz kafka on video,

or we could hear his voice on tape or in radio features.
thank god we don't have any satellite images
of the crucifixion of golgotha.

we know that from the ancient poets,
it's been drummed in ad nauseam ever since:
can a weed help being a weed?
can the chaff help its chaff-like existence?
what can lambs do about
ending up on our dinner plates?
enzensberger taught us all this back in the sixties
when he defended the wolves,
so let us move on.
just like the simple is overwhelmed by the diverse,
but we know from british
and american laboratories,
that hate, envy and malevolence are
chemical processes,
that can be switched off,
says my friend and companion,
as we drive away from san francisco
cruising south to monterey and into salinas valley.

a story is playing on the radio.
it all started with the sport, going to the gym
every day,
she'd jog like she was crazy.
then she had her hair cut short.

we have three children.
no action between the sheets
in three months,
he doesn't touch her anymore,
because she's become too masculine.
her tight muscles, her short hair.
he doesn't deny frequenting the clubs.
the question that follows is understandable.
the program ends in three minutes
before the world news.
they're supposed to decide
whether they should get divorced.
if they do, he'll go abroad.
when she first set eyes on him all those years ago
she knew he was the love of her life.
the midday bells have started ringing.
the daily news follows.

we all know what we want:
gorging without calories,
violence without pain,
anger without hate,
talking without words,
silence with a din,
noise without sound,
travel without motion,
stagnation with speed,
running away to stay,

thinking without thought,
solitude without loneliness,
illness without suffering,
pure pleasure
without the flipside
death without dying.

dad, asks my ten-year-old son
at the station, how do letters
get into your mouth?
no idea, i answer
then he climbs on the train
and travels to kufstein
and we wave to each other,
and i stand there motionless for some time,
because i just don't feel like
leaving, and it's a few minutes
before i go into the station building
and buy a can that i drink right there,
a few drunken hobos are hanging around,
one of them looks at me,
staggering and mumbling under his breath,
and his buddy
tells me not to be mad at him.

and here, my dear ladies and gentlemen:
it's all just a trick, all false bottoms, illusions.
between the lines:

don't believe a word, not even a letter,
or a sentence, because it's all lies,
lies from beginning to end.
nothing has anything to do with anything,
a potato isn't a potato here,
and what you read and what you see
in this establishment,
is nothing more than noise and smoke:
forget it before you become entangled
in the snare,
in the dazzling lights, the dancing,
the legs and high kicks,
the clacking stiletto heels,
black hats flying in the air,
canes with ivory knobs,
all just fantasy,
intangible,
all a dream,
distant and unreal,
do not touch,
no touching,
no entry,
like earthly gardens
on a cinema screen.

if you feel dirty inside,
you want everything around you to be clean,
which is why i'm notorious

for scrubbing and vacuum cleaning,
edi tells me on his cell phone.
i'm in a good mood and as i make my way home
to my dirty flat that evening,
i wonder whether the opposite is also true.

a critical commentator
wrote in a column in the daily paper:
the privatization of austrian state-owned companies
has led to their disintegration.
even the good old mail service,
whose stolidity
often drove me mad
to the point of wishing
it were privatized,
is now going down this route
and therefore down the drain.
but that doesn't make me happy.
i do read it with a tinge of satisfaction though
and i immediately think of trieste.
why on earth does that make you think of trieste?
an old drinking buddy asks me,
who once worked for the mail service.
it's a long story, the connection
between trieste and the mail service.
yeah, yeah, says my buddy,
i'm not really interested anyway,
because it's monday tomorrow

and i'm drunk today
and ever since privatization
st monday's are no longer
an option.

she's a fantastic woman,
because you can take her anywhere
without feeling ashamed.
besides, she pays for her own food
and drink,
says the man with life experience.
what's more, i'd rather have rings on my fingers
than under my eyes,
he chuckles like a man of the world
twisting his thick wedding band,
before ordering a glass of white wine,
because it's early afternoon
and he doesn't drink
red before the evening.

the whole village has turned out,
all because it was mentioned
in a traveler's letter
twelve-hundred years ago:
cyreolu
was the first written documentation of the village
where computer-generated texts are being broadcast
through a loudspeaker on the square,

much to the amusement of all present.
similarly, printed rolls of paper
are spilling out of the open windows of the library
as if in a futuristic film.
sentence after sentence relating to the village,
flashing across the screens,
before being printed on paper
while a language transformer
relays the sentences
through the loudspeaker
across the village square
and even victor and roman are astounded
by their creation, the poetry computer,
which delights but also disconcerts
the village population.
random, victor later says in his familiar casual way,
chomsky, word pots, syntactic structures,
and the journalist who asked him for the computer's
blueprint, is slightly confused, roman
notices and clears his throat,
without uttering a word,
as is commonplace in the uplands.
victor savors this moment,
as the paper rolls continue
to spill out of the windows
and a few boisterous kids
spread them across the village square,
as the party starts breaking up and

people slowly go their separate ways
all in high spirits,
many disappearing into the surrounding inns and bars
to forget the massive computer-text assault
marking this 1200th anniversary.

letters cannot be
twisted and changed
in their form.
they have a right
to be used sensibly.
they have contributed greatly
to our acquaintance,
writes a german philology scholar
in the preface to his postdoctoral thesis.

in life, people strive only
to gain pleasure and
avoid pain,
says a television report from imst
in an exclusive interview with an insurance salesman,
who is consequently snubbed by
the top ten thousand
of the city's population.

at the bogen 84,
a bar for hard-nosed drinkers,
as inviting as a shabby old living room,

peter vonstadl is talking at
an art student, who accidentally strayed there.
i can't paint, says peter, just like
cavemen couldn't paint,
i mix my spit into the paints though,
so that my dna's in every picture.
i can't write poetry,
but then cavemen couldn't
write either.
their alphabet was
the sound,
the phoneme
and that's why no-one knows
what wonderful songs
they sang
in the forests
and on the waters.
this mad man brings such beautiful images to the
world,
thinks the art student and notices
right away
that his drinking companion is hoping for a refill.
he orders a bottle of beer and peter
jumps down from his bar stool
to thank him,
but loses his balance
and crashes to the floor,
but he doesn't hurt himself,

because peter never injures himself,
he's used to the hard life
in the forests of mötz
where he grew up.

peter has the healthy instinct
of a forest dweller,
even when it comes to his art,
believes the art student,
as peter insists you should never desperately
want a poem, no, you must allow it to appear
and, for a truly precious poem, you can only
place your hand at its disposal,
as you watch it emerge
from your pen.
quite still and quiet, and if you're
a religious man like me,
full of humility.
you can't think poems up in your head,
you can only allow them to happen,
peter rants on and on
as the art student bids him farewell
feeling slightly overwhelmed
in these surroundings,
after all, he's from a good home.
god be with you, peter shouts after him
thanking him for the second bottle of beer
the student had bought him,

and see you soon,
peter calls out to the door.
it won't be more than a blink of an eye
before we bump into each other again
in the caves and forests of mötz,
peter mumbles on,
before taking another swig from the bottle.

in lowell you can still read the following quote:
a haiku with its seventeen syllables
is a small box.
once inside it, you are as free as a bird,
a zen-buddhist once told gary snyder
and harry redl.

we can operate,
says the eye specialist,
who gives me a letter
for my employer,
confirming i shouldn't
work on a computer.
the operation would have
a fifty-fifty chance of success,
he said,
but problems would definitely persist.
on my way back to work
i drop in at the café central
feeling down,

hoping i don't bump into
anyone i know.
i order a mineral water
and ask myself
what to make of
this doctor's letter.

because i just can't seem to let go
of the copyright issue,
i write a letter to nuremberg
and to the albertina in vienna.
i ask whether albrecht dürer
was really the first artist
to sign his work.
as soon as i've posted the letter
i no longer care whether i get a reply.
my enquiries about copyright
seem completely pointless, at least at that moment.
so victor switches his writing computer back on
again,
for which the copyright question also remains unclear:
in bad weather the priest mocks
the tourism association.
several big-chested women
fear the culture committee.
in the swinging sixties
suicidal
all degenerate writers from zirl.

and so on
and so forth
and victor slaps his thigh
and roman clears his throat
while i promise myself
never to work
on a computer again.

everything i know,
i know from others.
it says in a family history from trieste
in which claudio magris imagines
he is reading to giorgio voghera.

it's sunday morning.
outside it's bitterly cold.
the sun hangs obliquely in the sky.
i'm at home drinking coffee
when i feel my dead father's
hand resting on my shoulder.
plain sentences at last,
i say to him,
and my father
invites me for an early drink.
i put on my coat,
climb in the car,
and we savor a quiet beer together,
before he says his goodbyes

and i walk through the village,
thinking this day is saved,
but knowing it's downhill from here.
tomorrow's monday anyway,
when it's all about pretending
to be busy again,
but that's the parting of the ways,
it's what keeps us moving.

everything is mysterious
not just pain,
and on judgment day
the completely other
will bear witness to
all the wrongs
he dumped on us.

in 1964 linuccia, a confident
of giorgio voghera, appeared
at the einaudi publishing house
and handed in the manuscript for il segreto,
but he didn't say
who had given it to him.
it was to remain a secret,
a mystery,
the copyright.

even though some in san marco knew,
people were generally happy to believe
that the book entitled il segreto
was written by anonimo triestino.

Trieste 2004

Elias Schneitter

was born and grew up in
Zirl in Tyrol, Austria. After
completing his schooling in
Stams, he had a variety of
jobs, working in souvenirs,
as an office clerk, a canoeing teacher in Sturgeon Lake
- Minnesota, a project manager for Ho-Ruck, a social
program for former inmates, and as an employee for
the Austrian social security system. Today, he works as
a freelance author. He is co-founder of the international
literature festival "sprachsalz" in Hall, Tyrol and head of
the small publishing house "edition-baes".

His first publications started appearing from 1974,
mainly in literary magazines (Fenster, Rampe, wespenest,
protokolle, projektil) and as radio plays. His first book
was published in 1979 (geflügelte worte). In 2014, he
was presented with the Kathy Acker Award for his com-
mitment to promoting international literature, above all,
between the USA and the German-speaking world.